Picture perfect . . . or camera crazy?

When the class lined up for lunch, I couldn't believe how messy everyone looked. All the boys were dirty and rumpled.

Elizabeth's dress looked wrinkled, but it wasn't dirty. I was glad.

My outfit was spotless. Lila still looked perfect too. I had wanted Lila's dress to get messed up before, but now I was glad that someone else was trying to look nice for our class picture.

But we still had to get through lunch.

Bantam Books in the SWEET VALLEY KIDS series

CLASS PICTURE DAY!

Written by
Molly Mia Stewart

Created by
FRANCINE PASCAL

Illustrated by
Marcy Ramsey

BANTAM BOOKS
NEW YORK · TORONTO · LONDON · SYDNEY · AUCKLAND

RL 2, 005-008

CLASS PICTURE DAY!
A Bantam Book / March 1997

*Sweet Valley High® and Sweet Valley Kids® are
registered trademarks of Francine Pascal.*

Conceived by Francine Pascal.

*Produced by Daniel Weiss Associates, Inc.
33 West 17th Street
New York, NY 10011.*

Cover art by Wayne Alfano.

ISBN: 0-553-48335-8

Published simultaneously in the United States and Canada

*Bantam Books are published by Bantam Books, a division of Bantam
Doubleday Dell Publishing Group, Inc. Its trademark, consisting of the
words "Bantam Books" and the portrayal of a rooster, is Registered in the
U.S. Patent and Trademark Office and in other countries. Marca
Registrada. Bantam Books, 1540 Broadway, New York, New York 10036.*

PRINTED IN THE UNITED STATES OF AMERICA

OPM   0 9 8 7 6 5 4 3 2 1

To Lauren Marie Santini

CHAPTER 1

Surprise

I knew when I woke up this morning that today was going to be special. Our teacher, Mrs. Otis, promised to have a surprise for us first thing in the morning. As my twin sister, Elizabeth, and I walked into room 203 at Sweet Valley Elementary, I wondered what it would be.

"Hey, Jessica," Elizabeth whispered. "Mrs. Otis said we're going to write letters today."

I froze. "No! That can't be her surprise."

"I think it sounds like fun," Elizabeth said.

I twirled my finger in a circle next to my ear to show her I thought she was crazy. "You're weird, Lizzie."

"No, I mean it," Elizabeth replied. "You're good at writing notes. Maybe you'll be good at writing letters too."

"You're right. It'll be a cinch." I hurried to my desk. "But I still don't think that's the surprise. Mrs. Otis said it would be *special*."

"What else could it be?" Elizabeth asked.

"Maybe it's a field trip," I said.

"Or a party," Elizabeth said, smiling.

That's it—a party! A party with games and prizes and . . . pizza. I closed my eyes and thought of pepperoni pizza slices. Lots of them. "A pizza party!" I exclaimed.

"With lots of cheese. And ice cream for dessert." Elizabeth licked her lips.

"Yum! Make-your-own sundaes!" I said.

Elizabeth giggled. "Oh, boy! I hope you're right."

By the way, my name is Jessica Wakefield. I am seven years old. I usually don't look forward to school. My twin sister, Elizabeth, loves school—*everything* about it. Even homework.

Yuck! Not me. I try to get Elizabeth to do my homework.

I like to pass notes to my friends. I like lunch. And I love recess. Especially jumping rope. I'm the best rope jumper in the class. Elizabeth likes to play tag and dodgeball. *Boy* sports.

Elizabeth and I are identical twins. I have blue-green eyes and long blond hair with bangs. Elizabeth does too. But just because we look alike doesn't mean we *think* alike.

There's only one Jessica Wakefield. And that's me! My name will be in flashing lights someday. Maybe I'll be on TV. I want to be a famous singer or a movie star!

Elizabeth wants to be a teacher, or maybe a professional soccer player. She can play soccer as well as the boys do. She's so good, she plays on their team.

Boys—double yuck! I try to stay away from them. They're so dumb!

Mrs. Otis tapped on her desk. "Class, sit down. I have the surprise I told you about."

Elizabeth and I dashed into our chairs. Shoes scraped. Book bags thunked down. Winston Egbert was walking backward and stumbled into Eva Simpson's lap.

"Ouch!" Eva yelled. She shoved him onto the floor.

Winston toppled over and groaned and moaned. Everyone laughed.

"Way to go, Winston," Jerry McAllister said.

Mrs. Otis gave Winston a warning look.

Winston can be really funny sometimes. He usually makes me laugh. Only now he was making Mrs. Otis mad. If Mrs. Otis got too mad, she wouldn't tell us about the surprise.

"Sit down, Winston," I whispered.

Winston dropped down into the seat in front of mine. Then he turned and winked at me. I kicked the bottom of his desk until he turned back around.

Charlie Cashman plunked into his seat and burped.

Gross! Winston and Charlie are two of the reasons I don't like boys. Sometimes I wish they'd disappear and never come back.

5

Mrs. Otis sighed. "Class, settle down, please. I have something very exciting for you."

I glanced around the room. Elizabeth's eyes were really wide. Winston leaned forward on his elbows. Charlie even closed his mouth.

I could almost smell the pepperoni. We were going to have a party. I knew it!

"We're going to learn how to write letters," Mrs. Otis said. She picked up a piece of chalk.

I groaned. Was Elizabeth right? Did Mrs. Otis think letter writing was a surprise?

"We have some special friends to write to," Mrs. Otis said, pulling out a big cardboard box. She had covered it with paper so it looked like a post office mailbox.

Elizabeth was looking at Mrs. Otis with a big smile. I could almost hear her brain ticking. She probably couldn't wait to get started.

"I talked to a teacher in Alaska," Mrs. Otis said. "We're going to be writing to the students in her class."

Alaska. Eskimo kids? What was Mrs. Otis talking about?

Mrs. Otis pulled out a big brown envelope. "The teacher's name is Mrs. Gazak. She sent us a picture of her class." Mrs. Otis held up a large photo. "I'm going to put this on the bulletin board so everyone can get a closer look. Each student sent an individual picture too."

Todd raised his hand.

"Yes, Todd?"

"Do they play soccer in Alaska?" Todd asked.

"That's a good question." Mrs. Otis smiled. "When you write your letter, you can ask your pen pal."

I strained to see the picture. There

was lots of white everywhere—snow. The kids were all standing in it. They had on big, heavy parkas, hats, and gloves. A couple of kids wore furry coats and hats.

"Is that a real dogsled in the picture?" Kisho Murasaki asked.

Mrs. Otis nodded. "Yes. And that's a real live moose standing in the back."

"Wow!" everyone said at once.

Is the moose the class pet? I wondered.

"First we're going to talk about letter writing," Mrs. Otis said. "Then we'll choose our pen pals." Our teacher tacked the picture on the bulletin board. "And by the way, be sure to dress your best for picture day tomorrow," she said. "We'll

8

include our pictures with our letters."

We all knew that the next day was class picture day at Sweet Valley Elementary. I love to get dressed up! Elizabeth and I were planning to wear matching outfits so everyone would have to look at our name bracelets to tell us apart.

We might even fool Mom or Dad or our older brother, Steven.

I wanted to stand next to my friends in the picture. My best friends, besides Elizabeth, are Lila Fowler and Ellen Riteman. Elizabeth's best friends are Todd Wilkins and Amy Sutton. She could stand next to them in the picture.

Mrs. Otis's surprise was OK. Getting pen pals from Alaska was better than just plain letter writing. But I still wished we were having a party. I looked at the picture on the bulletin board. I couldn't wait for our picture day! Maybe we'd impress our pen pals with a super photo.

Then I noticed Winston's cowlick standing straight up and Ellen's puke green tights.

How could our class picture be as good as the one from Alaska? They had snow, a real dogsled, and a moose!

We had a couple of hamsters, a rabbit, and some weird *boys*.

CHAPTER 2
Mooseboy

Mrs. Otis wrote the word *salutation* on the board. "This word comes from the word *salute*. It means 'greeting,'" Mrs. Otis said. "When you write a letter, always put the date at the top of the page." She copied down the date. "Then write your salutation. For example: 'Dear Mary.'" She glanced at me, then Lila. "It's the same way you girls start your notes to each other."

"Yeah, *girls*," Charlie teased.

"Now, I want you to practice by copying the letter on the board,"

Mrs. Otis said. "While you're working, everyone can take turns coming up and looking at the picture of your pen pals. We'll start with this row."

I tried copying from the board, but it was hard to concentrate with everyone moving around and whispering. Some of the kids were arguing over who they would get to write to. It wasn't fair. I hadn't even gotten a chance to look yet.

"Look at that girl," Ellen said. "I hope she's my pen pal."

"I hope I don't get a girl," Charlie said. "I'd rather write to the dog."

Jerry hooted with laughter. "Or that big moose."

I tried again to copy the words from the board. My pencil slipped. My *d* turned into an *o* and I had to erase it.

Would it ever get to be my turn?

"Jessica, Elizabeth, Todd, and Winston, you can come up," Mrs. Otis said.

I jumped up so fast, I almost knocked over my desk. Elizabeth and I hurried to the front.

"Gee, look at that moose," Todd said.

"It's beautiful," Elizabeth said. Elizabeth loves animals. I like them OK, except for the ones that smell.

"And all that snow," Winston said. "It must be ten feet deep."

"It can't be ten feet deep, Winston. It would be over their heads," Elizabeth said.

I leaned closer to the picture. There were twenty-two kids in the class. Some of them looked like Eskimos, but most of them looked just like us. Twelve boys. Only ten girls. I felt sorry for the girls. Being outnumbered by boys must be awful.

"Who do you want to write to?" I asked Elizabeth.

"I don't care," Elizabeth said. "It'll

just be fun to find out how they live."

"Yeah. Do they really live in igloos?" Winston asked.

"I don't think so," Elizabeth said.

"Hey, look at that guy," Todd said. "With that dark fur coat and hat, he looks like the moose."

I looked at the boy. He was frowning. He did look like a moose. Or maybe a bear.

A scary grizzly bear.

I shivered.

Charlie is pretty scary too. Maybe he would want to write to him.

"I bet he knows a lot about scaring girls," Winston said.

I ignored him and pointed to the prettiest girl in the picture. "I hope she'll be my pen

14

pal," I whispered to Elizabeth.

"I bet she's a real Eskimo," Elizabeth said.

"I wonder if she has an Eskimo doll," I said.

Elizabeth grinned. "That's something you can ask in your letter."

I was getting excited. "Maybe she'd even send me one of her dolls. I could send her one of mine too. We could trade!"

"Maybe we can go visit them," Elizabeth said, and pointed to Alaska on the globe.

I pointed to California, where we live. It seemed like a long way to Alaska. "We'd have to fly," I said.

"We could ride in a dogsled when we get there," Elizabeth said.

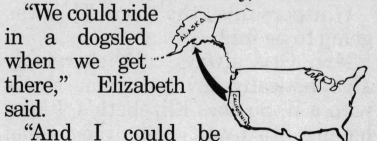

"And I could be

15

snow queen of Alaska." I twirled around and curtsied.

"OK, kids, sit down," Mrs. Otis said. She put the big cardboard mailbox in the middle of the room. "Now we're going to choose pen pals."

"I want the pretty Eskimo girl!" Lila yelled.

I glared at Lila.

"I want the boy in the white fur suit," Todd said. "He looks like a polar bear."

"Shhh," Mrs. Otis said. "To be fair, I've put all the letters inside this mailbox. Each of you will draw out a letter. The student whose letter you draw will be your pen pal."

Whispers filled the room. This was going to be fun!

Mrs. Otis always calls everybody alphabetically. My last name starts with a *W*. So does Elizabeth's. I hate having to wait all the time.

Elizabeth and I were going to be almost last!

"Look. This boy's name is Ben," Charlie said, opening his letter. "He says he goes ice fishing all the time."

Winston opened his letter and waved it in the air. "Sam Huch. He races dogsleds."

All the boys crowded around to read Sam's letter.

"I picked a girl named Becky Hope," Lila said. She flashed Becky's picture. Becky had red hair and big green eyes. "She likes to play dress-up," Lila squealed.

Lila got a good pen pal. I chewed my bottom lip. What if my pen pal was weird?

"I got a girl named Hillary," Ellen said. "Isn't she pretty?" Ellen held up a photo of a girl with dark hair, dark eyes, and a big smile.

If I couldn't get the pretty Eskimo

girl, I would have wanted Hillary as my pen pal.

Amy Sutton went to the mailbox. She came back beaming. "Look, this girl is a real Eskimo."

My heart sank. Amy had picked the pen pal I wanted!

Who was left?

When Elizabeth and I were finally called, we went to the box to draw. "Good luck," I whispered.

"You too," she said.

"Since you're twins, you can pick at the same time," Mrs. Otis said.

"One, two, *three!*" Elizabeth and I counted.

Then we stuck our hands in the box.

Elizabeth grabbed an envelope and tore it open. "I got a girl named Sally Poe."

I opened mine and suddenly felt sick. It was the boy with the dark fur suit and hat.

Mooseboy.

"Hey, let me see." Elizabeth tried to pull it out of my hand.

I snatched the letter back.

"Jessica!"

I slipped it to her. "It's Mooseboy, Liz."

"Mooseboy?" Elizabeth asked. She opened the letter. "His name is Bob Burdett," she read. "He says that at recess, the class goes cross-country skiing. He likes ice fishing and hunting bears with his dad."

"Hunting bears? Gross." This boy wouldn't have an Eskimo doll. And I bet he would make fun of me for wanting to be a movie star. I grabbed Elizabeth's hand. "Will you trade pen pals with me?"

Elizabeth studied the picture. "Sure."

Mrs. Otis was copying the names of everyone and their pen pal on the board. She wrote Elizabeth's name beside Sally Poe's.

"Mrs. Otis," I asked softly, "can Elizabeth and I trade?"

Mrs. Otis frowned. "No, I'm sorry, Jessica. Part of the idea behind writing to pen pals is to get to know people who are different from you." She copied my name beside Bob Burdett's.

Suddenly Charlie was standing behind me. "Hey, *Jessica* picked a *boy*," he yelled.

"Ooh! Jessica's got a boyfriend!" Jerry shouted.

I walked back to my desk and tried to figure out how I could hide underneath it. Mrs. Otis's surprise was definitely *not* a nice surprise at all!

I started counting the minutes until picture day.

At least *that* would be fun.

CHAPTER 3

The Argument

As soon as Elizabeth and I got home, I ran past Mom and headed toward the stairs.

"Hi, girls. Don't you want a snack?" Mom was sitting at the dining room table, working on a project for her interior decorating class. She says she likes her school, but I don't see why. She has lots of homework and no recess.

"Later, Mom!" I shouted. "Come on, Liz. Let's pick out our clothes for picture day."

Elizabeth followed me up to our

room. As usual, her side was neat and clean. I had clothes and dolls lying everywhere. I kicked my sneakers under my bed and opened the closet door.

"This will be perfect," I said, pulling out our nicest dresses. They were yellow with blue flowers. "We can wear our shiny black shoes."

"I don't want to wear a dress," Elizabeth said. She pulled out our new shorts and matching tops. "I like these better. I could still play kickball at recess."

"No," I insisted. "We *have* to wear dresses in our class picture."

Elizabeth put her hands on her hips. "We don't usually wear pretty dresses to school. We should dress like we always do."

"But Mrs. Otis said to look *nice,*" I argued. Why was Elizabeth being so difficult?

"We'll look nice in shorts too," Elizabeth said. "Besides, I can't kick a ball in those black shoes." Elizabeth sounded angry. Her cheeks were turning red.

"You and your dumb boy games," I said. "It's picture day! Can't you *not* play soccer for one day?"

Just then our older brother, Steven, poked his head in through the door. "What are you two squirts screaming about?"

"Jessica wants us to wear our frilly yellow dresses to school," Elizabeth said.

"Our teacher said to look nice for our class pictures!" I yelled. "We have to send them to our pen pals in Alaska."

Suddenly Steven grinned.

Uh-oh. I shouldn't have said anything about the pen pals. Steven is always finding ways to tease me and Elizabeth.

"Oh, Jess, I heard about your boyfriend," Steven said. "You want to look pretty for Mooseboy."

"I do not!" Having a boy pen pal was bad enough, but getting teased was even worse. "How do you know about it anyway?" I asked.

"Charlie Cashman told me on the bus," Steven said. "Wait till I tell him you're dressing up for your new boyfriend!"

I clenched my hands by my sides to keep from hitting Steven. "I am not!" I yelled.

"What is all this shouting about?" Mom asked as she came up the steps.

"We're supposed to look our best for picture day tomorrow," I said. "So I think we should wear our new yellow dresses."

"I want us to wear shorts!"

Elizabeth said angrily. "I can't play kickball in that dress."

"Jessica wants to look pretty for her boyfriend," Steven added.

"Stop!" Mom said. "Steven, I want you to go downstairs."

Steven shrugged and walked away. When Mom turned her back, he puckered his lips and made a kissing sound. I lunged after him, but Mom stepped in front of me. "Let's talk, girls."

Elizabeth and I sat down on our beds.

"I know tomorrow is picture day," Mom said. "And Elizabeth, I understand it's hard to play kickball in a dress. But I'm planning to send this picture to all your relatives and I would like for you to look nice."

"But Mom!" Elizabeth argued.

I grinned. At least something was working out for me that day.

"Just this once, I want you both to

wear the dresses," Mom said softly. "Elizabeth, why don't you bring a change of clothes and your sneakers to school and change into them at recess?"

Elizabeth looked sullen but nodded.

"Now, come downstairs and have some ice cream."

"OK," Elizabeth said, and smiled at me. "Race you."

We both ran down the stairs. Elizabeth beat me. I didn't care. I was just glad we were wearing our new dresses for our class pictures.

"What are you going to write in your letter to Moo—um, I mean, your pen pal?" Elizabeth asked as we ate our ice cream.

"I don't want to talk about it. I'll lose my appetite!" I said.

I decided to think about class picture day instead. I could see myself all dressed up, smiling at the camera. Bright lights were shining down on me. People were clapping and calling my name, just the way they would if I were on TV. Even Lila Fowler wouldn't look as pretty as me in my new dress.

Class picture day was going to be picture perfect!

CHAPTER 4
Movie-Star Gorgeous

"We look bee-*yoo*-tiful," I said to Elizabeth as I twirled in front of the mirror the next morning. "Don't you just love these new socks?" Our socks were yellow with little blue bows, and they matched our dresses perfectly.

Elizabeth shrugged as she stuffed her sneakers into her book bag. "I'll be glad when the pictures are over. I hope they're the first thing, so we don't have to stay neat all day. I want to play kickball during recess."

I rolled my eyes. Elizabeth doesn't mind getting dirty. I hate it.

Tilting my head sideways, I smiled at my reflection in the mirror. Should I show my teeth when I smiled, or keep my mouth closed? I turned with my left side facing the mirror, then with my right side. "Which side of me looks best?" I asked my sister.

"You look the same both ways," Elizabeth said impatiently as she started toward the door.

"Hey, don't forget your dress shoes," I said. "We have to match perfectly."

Elizabeth took off her sandals and put on her shiny black shoes. "There. Are you happy now?"

"Yes! We're going to look gorgeous, like movie stars."

This time Elizabeth rolled *her* eyes. But she smiled at the same time.

We hurried downstairs together. Steven was in the kitchen, arguing with Mom. "I can't believe you're making me wear a tie," Steven said. "I look like a dork in these pants. None of the other fourth-grade boys will be dressed up."

"Steven, what would Grandma think if I let you wear those ripped jeans you had picked out?"

Elizabeth and I giggled.

"You look like a teacher, Steven," I said in a teasing voice.

"Shut up!" Steven yelled, and ran toward me.

I hid behind the couch, laughing at the mad face Steven was making. "Be careful, or your face will freeze like that," I called. "*Then* how will your picture look?"

"Not as ugly as yours!" Steven yelled back.

"Time to go, kids," Mom said. "Now I want everyone to act as nice as they look."

That was easy for me. But I knew there was no way Steven could act as nice as he looked. After all, he's *Steven*.

When we got to school, everyone was talking and pointing at everyone else. For a minute I thought I'd walked into the wrong classroom. I even double-checked the number on the door to make sure it was 203.

"Look, Lizzie, Winston Egbert has on a white shirt and a tie."

Elizabeth laughed. "He must have put hair spray in his hair. His cowlick isn't sticking up as much as it usually does."

Even though Winston was dressed up, he still looked funny. He was holding his breath so his cheeks ballooned out. All he needed was a red nose, and he'd really look like a clown.

"Even Todd and Jerry are

31

dressed up," I pointed out. All the boys had their hair combed neatly. I hardly recognized them.

"You look great," Amy said as she ran up to Elizabeth.

"You too," Elizabeth said. "I like that red skirt."

Lila waltzed over. "What do you think of my new dress?" she asked.

"It's pretty," I said. Lila is one of my best friends, but sometimes she can be a snob. Her dress was made out of some kind of frilly pink material with a big bow in the middle of the back.

Lila looked like a princess. It wasn't fair!

Lila brushed the soft fabric with her fingers. "I'm wearing it in my cousin's wedding next month. How do I look?"

Before I could reply, Charlie Cashman walked in, wearing a suit and tie. I giggled.

"Don't laugh," Charlie said. "At least I'm not dressing up to impress some pen pal."

"Yeah, Jessica, are you trying to look good for your *boyfriend?*" Jerry asked.

I glared at Jerry. "Mooseboy is *not* my boyfriend," I said.

Then Mrs. Otis came in the door. Even she was wearing a fancy dress. "Good morning, class," Mrs. Otis said.

Everyone dove into their seats.

"First we're going to head over to the library," Mrs. Otis announced.

I waved my hand.

"Yes, Jessica?" Mrs. Otis said.

"When are we getting our pictures taken?" I asked.

"Yeah, I want to take off this stupid tie," Charlie said.

"I'm sorry," Mrs. Otis said. "But the kindergartners and the first-graders have to go first."

Everyone groaned.

"You'll have to be patient," Mrs. Otis said. "Now, let's line up and go to the library. We're going to do some research on Alaska. Then we'll work on our letters to our pen pals."

Elizabeth was line leader, of course. So I got in line next to Lila.

"I can't get my dress messed up," Lila said as we walked down the hall. "I have to wear it in my cousin's wedding."

"You already told us," I said.

"I'm going to be the flower girl," she continued, as though she hadn't even heard me.

"Uh-huh," I said in a bored voice. Whenever Lila acts snobby, I usually try to ignore her. So that's what I did.

"I can't wait to write to my pen pal," Lila said when we got to the library and settled down at a table. "She'll just love my picture. I bet they don't have dresses this pretty in Alaska."

I flipped the pages of the encyclopedia. Reading about shark fishing in Alaska was better than listening to Lila! I looked over at Elizabeth, who was already taking notes from a big book on Alaska. She'd probably have a huge report written by the time library period was over.

"I'm going to ask Mrs. Otis if I can stand in the middle of the class for the picture," Lila said. "Since I've got the fanciest dress, I should be in the center."

I wanted to yank the bow out of Lila's hair. Elizabeth and I looked just as pretty as Lila did. Since I was stuck with the worst pen pal in the class, shouldn't *I* be the star of the class picture?

CHAPTER 5

Blue Paint Ocean

"OK, class, put away your notes from the library," Mrs. Otis said when we got back to room 203. "We need to finish our social studies projects."

"Mrs. Otis, when are we going to get our pictures taken?" I asked.

Mrs. Otis smiled. "Be patient, Jessica. They'll call us when they're ready."

"You'll probably break the camera anyway," Charlie whispered.

"Very funny," I said,

making a face. "I won't have to, 'cause it'll already be broken from *your* picture."

Mrs. Otis gave Charlie and me warning looks. Then she looked at the whole class. "You did such a good job making your papier-mâché globes the other day. Now it's time to paint them." Mrs. Otis pointed to some pots of paint on her desk. "I have all the colors you'll need for oceans and lakes, land, mountains, and forest areas."

Lila bounced up and down in her chair and waved her hand. I thought she was going to fall out of her chair. "But Mrs. Otis," Lila whined, "what if I get paint on my dress? My daddy will be *sooo* upset."

Mrs. Otis tapped her chin in thought. "You'll just have to be very careful. Everyone needs to wear paint smocks today." I didn't think that would work. Some of the kids in the class were awfully clumsy.

"Can't we paint tomorrow instead?" I asked. "We can wear our old clothes. Then it won't matter if we spill anything."

Mrs. Otis shook her head. "Our social studies projects are going to be displayed at the PTA meeting tomorrow night. If we paint them tomorrow, they won't have time to dry."

We put on our smocks and found our globes. Mrs. Otis had covered the long art tables with newspapers and the floor with big sheets of plastic.

I think she expected us to make a mess.

I smoothed down my smock and made sure it covered every inch of my dress. I slid my feet under the table so paint couldn't drip on my brand-new socks.

Lila snatched the longest smock and frowned. "It's already got paint on it."

"That paint's dry," Elizabeth said.

"It won't come off on you."

Mrs. Otis placed plastic paint cups and brushes on the table. Everyone started grabbing them all at once. I waited until things had settled down. Maybe the boys didn't care if they got messy, but *I* wanted to stay pretty. Secretly I wished that the paint on Lila's smock was wet. Even though she was wearing the prettiest dress in Sweet Valley, I wanted to be the star of picture day.

"At least we get to do something exciting," Jerry said. "Dressing up for picture day was bad enough, and going to the library was *bo*-ring."

"Yeah, who wants to read the encyclopedia?" Charlie said.

"I thought it was neat," Elizabeth said. "I didn't know the Alaskan Eskimos came from Siberia."

"Sib-*where*-ia?" Ellen asked, and we all laughed.

"Do you know how cold it gets in Alaska?" Todd asked.

"No, how cold?" Elizabeth wondered.

"Minus seventy degrees," Todd said.

I shivered just thinking about it.

"I guess that's why Mooseboy wears that big furry coat," Winston said.

I ignored Winston and painted the land on my globe brown, being careful not to get paint on my hands. Jerry and Charlie were slopping paint onto their globes. The blue and brown paint was running together. You couldn't tell the oceans from the land or the mountains.

"I wonder if Mooseboy killed a bear and made that coat himself," Charlie said.

"Maybe Jessica can ask him when she writes her love letter," Jerry replied.

If it hadn't been class picture day, I might've thrown my paintbrush at Jerry.

"I'm *not* writing a love letter," I said. "I can't help it if my pen pal's a boy."

"You picked Mooseboy on purpose," Jerry said.

"I did not," I said.

"Did too," Jerry teased.

"Oh yeah?" I picked up my paintbrush and pretended I was going to throw it at him. Jerry jumped back and bumped into Lila, who bumped into Charlie. Charlie's elbow hit the jar of blue paint.

I yelped and jumped back as an ocean of blue paint came flowing toward me.

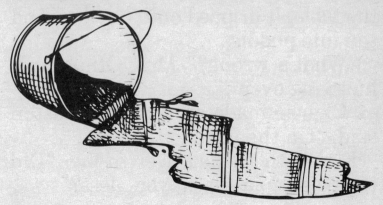

CHAPTER 6

The Explosion

"Watch out!" Lila screamed.

I was frozen in place, staring at the growing pool of blue paint. It was going everywhere!

Charlie grabbed the paint tub and turned it upright. Blue paint streaked the table. It dripped onto the floor and ran into puddles.

"What's wrong?" Mrs. Otis asked, hurrying over.

"Charlie made an ocean," Winston said. "On the floor."

Elizabeth rushed over to me. "Did the paint splatter on you, Jess?"

We both examined my dress, looking up and down for any paint spots.

"It looks OK," Elizabeth said.

"Yeah, the paint missed me," I said, relieved.

Mrs. Otis piled extra newspapers on the floor to soak up the paint.

The secretary from the office knocked on the door and poked her head inside the room. She gave Mrs. Otis a funny look when she saw her on her hands and knees in the middle of a pile of blue newspapers. "Mrs. Otis?"

Mrs. Otis looked up from her spot on the floor. "Yes?"

"The photographer's running a little behind," the secretary said. "He'll get to your class after lunch."

Mrs. Otis checked her watch. "Finish up your globes, class, and we'll do a science project next."

As everyone put the last strokes of

color on their globes, I took off my smock and went to my desk. I was grateful social studies was over. Science had to go better.

Everyone settled down in their seats. "Let's take a look at Alaska," Mrs. Otis said. She pointed to a big map on the wall. "Notice the long chain of volcanoes. Since the sixteenth century, forty-one volcanoes have erupted there."

"Ooh." Winston made a weird face. His eyes looked buggy.

"Cool," Eva said.

"For our experiment," Mrs. Otis said, "I've made a volcano shell out of plaster of paris."

"Wow!" Charlie said.

"Can we see it?" Todd asked.

Mrs. Otis held it up. It looked like a little white mountain with a hole in the middle.

"Now we're going to make a

mixture for the insides of the vol-cano," Mrs. Otis said.

"Can we watch it erupt?" Andy Franklin asked.

Mrs. Otis smiled. "That's the whole idea."

Everyone leaned forward in their seats.

"We'll be using vinegar, detergent, and baking soda," Mrs. Otis said. "I need some helpers."

Everyone raised their hands and waved them wildly, except me. No way was I going to get volcano slime on my dress!

"Todd, Elizabeth, and Ken, you come

up and help. The rest of you gather around the table so you can watch."

Everyone jumped up and crowded around the minivolcano. Charlie bullied his way to the front. Tom McKay and Ricky Capaldo tried to elbow him out. The table scraped as the boys jarred it. Julie Porter grabbed the volcano shell to keep it from sliding off the table.

"Please be still," Mrs. Otis said. "We don't want any more accidents before class pictures."

Elizabeth measured the vinegar and poured it in the middle.

"Whew! That stuff smells!" Jerry said.

We pinched our noses, and Charlie made a fake coughing sound.

"Now, add the detergent, Ken," Mrs. Otis said. Ken dumped the liquid detergent in the center. It turned into a thick blue-gray mixture.

"OK, Todd, add the baking soda," Mrs. Otis said.

Todd picked up the measuring spoon. "How much?"

"Six tablespoons," Mrs. Otis said.

Todd held the spoon over the volcano opening and tilted the baking soda box sideways.

"Wait!" Mrs. Otis said. "Don't pour the baking soda into the volcano!"

But it was too late. As Todd shook the box, lots of baking soda came pouring out. It went right into the mixture. The volcano gurgled and bubbled. The mixture sizzled and spewed.

Then it exploded!

CHAPTER 7

Recess Monkeys

I jumped back and bumped into Julie. She bumped into Amy. Amy bumped into Ken. Ken bumped into Ricky. Ricky bumped into Ellen.

We were like dominos knocking against one another.

"Eek!" Lila screamed.

"Awesome!" Charlie shouted.

"Is that the way a volcano really erupts?" Lois Waller asked.

The volcano mixture oozed and splattered onto the desk. *Pop! Whiz!* It fizzed over the table edge, plopping and dripping onto the floor.

"Gross!" Caroline Pearce yelled.

"Get some paper towels!" Mrs. Otis called.

Elizabeth and Todd ran to get the paper towels and handed them to her. Mrs. Otis pressed the paper towels on the swirls of fake lava.

"That was *sooo* neat!" Winston said. He grabbed a mop to clean up the thick goop. But instead of helping, he ended up smearing the mixture across the floor.

"Be careful," Lila warned. "You're going to get it on my nice shoes!"

Winston whirled around to make a face at Lila, but he caught the mop handle on his shirtsleeve. We heard a loud ripping sound as the mop tore his sleeve.

Mrs. Otis pushed her hair back from her face. She looked frazzled. Her dress looked really rumpled too. She wiped a glob of fake lava off the counter. "Sorry, kids. It wasn't supposed to explode like that."

"Luckily it didn't splatter all over my new dress," Lila said. She was standing about ten feet from the table. "If I'd known we were doing all this messy stuff, I would have worn a raincoat."

"I think we should go out to recess," Mrs. Otis said, sighing. "Maybe while we're outside a magic fairy will come in and clean up our room." She looked as if she really hoped that would happen.

I scanned the class. It looked as if we'd had both a tornado *and* a volcano. Piles of blue newspapers, fake volcano lava, and paper towels were everywhere.

If I hadn't known better, I'd have thought some alien was trying to ruin picture day!

Mrs. Otis clapped her hands.

"Well, at least we have our PTA projects finished. Now let's go to recess, everyone."

We all raced for the door.

"Remember to be careful on the playground. We still have pictures this afternoon," Mrs. Otis warned.

Elizabeth grabbed her sneakers from her book bag.

"Aren't you going to change into your shorts too?" I asked.

"No. There isn't enough time. Besides, I'll be careful," Elizabeth said.

I hoped she was right.

"What do you want to play today?" Ellen asked me when we got to the playground.

Lila walked up beside us. "Let's play fairy-tale land. I'll be the queen and you guys can be the princesses."

I shook my head. "We're playing beauty pageant. You can be Miss California if you want."

"I'm going to be Miss America," Ellen said.

I smiled as brightly as the afternoon sun. "And I'll be Miss Universe."

Lila turned up her nose. "I'm tired of playing beauty pageant. I think we should just stand here and talk so we don't mess up our clothes."

I didn't want to get dirty either, but I was really sick of Lila. "Playing beauty pageant is easy. We can just parade up and down the sidewalk," I suggested.

"I know. We could have a fashion show," Ellen said.

"Yeah," I agreed. I pretended to hold a camera in front of me. "Come on, act like you're a model and smile."

Lila and Ellen threw their arms out in silly poses and grinned. I made snapping sounds as if I were taking pictures. "Now you take one of me," I said.

This time Ellen pretended to take pictures. Lila and I posed the way models do on TV.

Just then a few kids ran by chasing a ball.

"Look at your sister," Lila said. "She's going to look awful for her picture."

Elizabeth and Amy were playing kickball with the boys. Was she getting dirt on her dress? I wanted to yell at Elizabeth to be careful, but she ran past me too fast.

"Her dress will be all dirty," Lila said. "And so will her hair."

I smoothed down my skirt and looked at the pretty blue flowers on it. *Lila was right,* I thought. Elizabeth was having a good time at recess, but when picture time came, she'd be sorry. I felt bad for her.

Wait a minute. I felt bad for *us*. Now we wouldn't look the same anymore.

Some of the boys were dangling upside down on the monkey bars. Winston's tie had come loose and was hanging lopsided.

"Hey, look at me!" Winston yelled. His hair was all spiked out, as usual. The hair spray hadn't lasted very long, because his cowlick was dancing in the wind. The rip in his sleeve had gotten bigger. Winston scratched under his arms, screeching like a monkey.

"Winston, you're a weirdo!" Lila yelled.

Eva and Caroline were turning a jump rope. Eva waved at me. "Jessica, do you want to jump rope after Julie?"

I turned around in time to see Julie trip over the rope.

She landed on her knee and started to cry. The bow on her left shoe came off too. When she stood up, big tears pooled in her eyes, and she dabbed at the scrape on her knee. She picked up the bow and tried to put it back on her shoe, but it wouldn't stay.

"Don't worry, Julie. Your shoes won't show in the picture," Eva said.

I didn't agree. Julie was one of the shortest girls in the class. If she was in the front row, her shoes might show. And what about her skinned knee?

"I don't think I'll jump rope today," I said.

When the class lined up for lunch, I couldn't believe how messy everyone looked. All the boys were dirty and rumpled. Charlie must have fallen, because the knees of his pants were muddy. Jerry's shirt had grass stains all over it. And Julie was limping.

Elizabeth's dress looked wrinkled,

but it wasn't dirty. I was glad. Elizabeth saw me and hurriedly smoothed out her dress. Lila and I squeezed in line.

My outfit was spotless. Lila still looked perfect too. I had wanted Lila's dress to get messed up before, but now I was glad that someone else was trying to look nice for our class picture.

But we still had to get through lunch.

CHAPTER 8
The Big Spill

Lunchtime dragged by as slowly as a turtle with a sprained ankle. Why couldn't we get our pictures taken before lunch? With so many kids crowding in the cafeteria at once and lining up at the same time, somebody almost always had an accident.

But it wouldn't be me. I would have to be extra careful. Nothing was going to ruin my picture.

I sat down next to Lila and took out my lunch: a turkey sandwich, carrot sticks, and pretzels. *Good*, I thought. *Nothing sloppy.*

But underneath my napkin was a grape juice box. *Oh, no!* I couldn't believe Mom would pack a grape juice box on picture day. Steven had probably put it in as a joke!

Well, I wasn't going to drink it. Grape juice would stain my dress! I laid the box on the table and decided to save it for home. I could drink water from the fountain instead.

"We're going to write our pen pals after lunch," Elizabeth said, crunching on her carrots. Amy and Todd sat down beside her. Eva and Ellen joined us too. Then Charlie pushed his way to the table. Yuck!

There was one open place across from me. *Maybe I should spread out my lunch so I won't get anything on my dress,* I thought.

"Hi, guys!" Winston said. He dropped into the empty chair and grinned. His hair was sticking out in a dozen different directions now.

"Have you decided what you're going to write in your letter?" Elizabeth asked Winston.

Winston took a bite of his peanut butter and mayonnaise sandwich. "I'll tell my pen pal how I can juggle. And how I can balance things on my nose."

"You can *not*," Lila said.

Winston wiggled his eyebrows. "Let me finish my lunch and I'll show you."

Mayonnaise oozed out the sides of Winston's sandwich and ran down his fingers. "That sandwich is so gross," I said.

Winston brings the same sandwich every day. Every day I tell him it's gross.

Winston laughed, spitting out bits of food. He hadn't fixed his tie, and the tear in his shirt looked awful.

I wondered if his mother would even *buy* his picture.

"I'm going to tell my pen pal about

my cousin's wedding," Lila said.

"Oh, who cares about some dumb wedding?" Charlie said. "I'm going to write about in-line skating."

"Watch me, everybody. *This* is the kind of stuff the kids in Alaska want to hear about," Winston said as he took his orange from his lunch box.

"What are you doing?" I asked him.

Winston tilted his head back. Then he put the orange on the tip of his nose. "I told you I could balance things on my nose."

"Don't show off," I said, looking at the clock. Three minutes till lunch was over. Three minutes to safety.

"Wow," Charlie said.

Elizabeth giggled.

Winston started waving his arms as if he could fly. The orange stayed put. "I can even walk and balance it on my nose."

"Don't, Winston," I said. "You're going to drop it."

"No, I won't," Winston said. He slowly pushed his chair back and stood up. The orange rolled a little bit, and Winston swayed, putting out his arms for balance.

Just then Eva took another bite of her apple and yelped. "My tooth!" Eva cried. "My tooth came out in the apple!"

Winston turned to look at Eva. The orange plopped down onto the table—and bounced on top of Elizabeth's grape juice box. The box got knocked on its side, and juice shot out through the straw as if it were coming from a squirt gun.

Elizabeth shrieked as the purple stain on her dress grew bigger and bigger.

CHAPTER 9

My Pen Pal Eats Mooseburgers?

"Winston, you ruined Elizabeth's dress!" Eva yelled.

This was disaster day, not picture day.

Elizabeth looked as if she was about to cry. I wanted to take her into the bathroom and hide there with her. I grabbed a napkin, ran to Elizabeth, and tried to wipe the stain off. "It's OK," I said.

Winston stood staring at the splatter of purple juice on Elizabeth's dress. He moved his mouth to speak, but nothing came out. Even Charlie kept his mouth shut for once.

The stain seemed to get bigger instead of smaller. "It's not coming out," Elizabeth said.

"Don't worry," I said. "We'll ask Mrs. Otis what to do."

Mrs. Otis wasn't happy at all. She gave Winston one of her sternest teacher looks and led our class back to room 203. "I want everyone to rest their heads on their desks," Mrs. Otis said. "We need to calm down." She looked at Elizabeth's dress. "I'm sorry, Elizabeth. I'm afraid I'll make it worse if I try to get the stain out. This dress will have to go to the cleaners."

Tears welled in Elizabeth's eyes and spilled over onto the stain. We couldn't get the dress to the cleaners and back before pictures.

"You still look nice, dear," Mrs. Otis said, handing Elizabeth a tissue. She went to the front of the class and picked up her chalk. "Now, I want everyone to take out a piece of paper and write a letter to your pen pal. Think of something interesting to tell your pen pal about yourself."

I stared at my blank piece of paper. I couldn't think of anything to say to Mooseboy. All I could think about was how picture day was spoiled because Elizabeth and I wouldn't look like twins anymore.

Then I had an idea. "Do you think I could color over the stain with Magic Marker?" I whispered to Elizabeth.

Elizabeth tucked a strand of blond hair behind her ear. "That might make it worse. And I don't know if marker would come out when Mom gets it cleaned."

My hopes sank. I glanced around the room. I *had* to think of a way to fix Elizabeth's dress. Then I spotted Lila's pearl necklace. It was beautiful. If Elizabeth wore a big necklace, it might cover the purple spot. I studied Lila's pearls. They would be just about the right length.

But Lila never shared. Especially her jewelry. And her dad had probably bought it just for the wedding. Besides, I wouldn't have a necklace, so Elizabeth and I wouldn't match.

"Let's keep working on our letters," Mrs. Otis said, looking right at me.

I grabbed my pencil and thought about Mooseboy's—I mean Bob's—letter. He liked to ice fish and hunt bears with his dad. I didn't know anything about ice fishing or bear hunting.

Dear Bob,
  Why do you like to ice fish and hunt bears?

Wait. If Mooseboy was like the boys in my class, he'd probably tell me all the gory details. I started over.

65

Dear Bob,
I know you like to ice fish and hunt bears. Everyone here calls you Mooseboy.

I groaned and crumpled the paper up. Then I got an idea.

Dear Bob,
Hi! My name is Jessica Wakefield. It's nice you like to ice fish and hunt bears.
Today is our class picture day. My twin sister Elizabeth and I dressed the same for it. But we don't look alike anymore. Winston dropped an orange and it made Elizabeth's grape juice squirt all over her dress. Other stuff happened too. Charlie knocked over blue paint and it spilled. Todd made our volcano blow up. Winston tore his shirt,

Julie skinned her knee, and Eva lost her tooth!

Our class is never this messy. Except for Winston. We have two hamsters named Thumbelina and Tinkerbell, and a bunny rabbit named Mr. Bunny.

Write back soon!
Sincerely,
Jessica Wakefield
Room 203

Suddenly I had a great idea how to make our picture look better. Maybe Elizabeth could hold Mr. Bunny in front of her stain. Then Elizabeth and I would be twins again, and I could *really* be the star of picture day!

CHAPTER 10

Who's Holding the Pets?

I waved my hand back and forth until I caught Mrs. Otis's attention. "I've got an idea, Mrs. Otis. Let's let Thumbelina, Tinkerbell, and Mr. Bunny be in our class picture."

"Well, I don't know . . . ," Mrs. Otis said.

"I think we should do it," Charlie said. "They're part of our class too."

I stared at Charlie in shock. Charlie and I never agree on anything!

"The kids from Alaska had their dogsled team in their picture," Elizabeth added.

"And that moose," I said.

Mrs. Otis smiled. "OK. If you guys can behave and keep them still."

She was going to let us do it! Hurray! Mrs. Otis is really a nice teacher.

"They should be calling us any minute for pictures," Mrs. Otis continued. "Take the animals out of their cages and get them ready." She handed me an animal brush so I could make them look good too.

The animals were probably going to look better than most of the kids in the class!

Todd and Eva got the hamsters. Elizabeth and Amy grabbed our class rabbit out of his cage. "Be  still, Mr. Bunny," I said, trying to brush his fur. "You're going to look beautiful." The rabbit wiggled and squirmed, but he looked adorable when I was finished.

"I want to hold Tinkerbell," Eva said.

"And I want to hold Thumbelina," Julie said.

Suddenly everyone started arguing over who'd get to hold the pets. But as they argued they let go of the animals. Tinkerbell ran under Mrs. Otis's desk, and Thumbelina scurried toward the back of the room. Several kids started chasing the hamsters.

"Oh, no," Mrs. Otis said.

Mr. Bunny must have sensed the commotion, because he got nervous and tried to wriggle away from Amy and Elizabeth. Amy held him tight.

A loud knock sounded at the door. "Excuse me, Mrs. Otis."

Everyone stopped and stared at the door. It was the principal! He frowned and looked around our messy room. "It's time for your class picture."

70

Finally, I thought. Thumbelina ran out from the corner, and Jerry dove for her. Todd snatched Tinkerbell just before she darted underneath the bookshelf.

"OK, let's go," Mrs. Otis said. She smoothed down her dress and paused to look at Winston. "Winston, that shirt will never do. Let me get you something else." She disappeared into her closet and came back with a flowered Hawaiian shirt in bright colors. It was the ugliest shirt I'd ever seen.

The whole class burst into laughter.

"Hey, this is cool," Winston said, grabbing the shirt. "It's me all the way."

I groaned and put my hands over my eyes, hoping that class picture day was just a bad dream.

CHAPTER 11

Show Time

There were bright camera lights in the auditorium. A short, bald man with a mustache was standing in front of a camera on a tripod. He motioned for us to come in.

"Hi, kids. We'll do the group shot first and then individuals."

"We can switch dresses for individuals," I told Elizabeth. She nodded. At least that wouldn't be so bad. "But we won't be twins in the group picture," I finished with a sigh.

The photographer narrowed his eyes at us. His long, wiry mustache twitched as he frowned. "What happened to you guys?"

"It's a long story," Mrs. Otis said.

Then I noticed the backdrop. It was just a plain blue sky and sunset. It looked like a photograph glued onto cardboard. The class from Alaska had real snow for their picture.

Winston made a dancing motion with his hands, as if he were doing the hula.

"Just because you have that Hawaiian shirt on doesn't mean you have to act like a coconut head," I said. Ellen laughed.

"No gum chewing, Charlie," Mrs. Otis warned. "Come on, class. The photographer has more classes to do after us."

"Mrs. Otis, we're all such a mess. Couldn't he come back another day?" I asked.

"*I'm* perfect today," Lila said,

twirling around in her dress. "Even more perfect than usual."

I glared at her. "Who cares? Look at everybody else." I turned to the photographer. "Can we do it another day?" I begged. "Look at Winston's shirt and Charlie's pants. And Julie lost the bow to her shoe."

"I skinned my knee too," Julie said, pointing at her hurt leg.

The photographer shook his head. "I'm afraid I can't. Now, let's get started."

Mrs. Otis passed out combs, and everyone tried to neaten up. Elizabeth and I stood in front of each other as though we were looking into a mirror and fixed each other's hair.

Elizabeth looked sad as she combed my hair. "At first I was really upset that Mom made me wear this dress," she said. "But then I saw how nice we looked, all dressed up alike. So I felt better." She frowned down at the stain on her dress. It looked like a big purple lake in the middle of a yellow field. "Now we don't look the same anymore. It's just not fair."

"Don't worry," I said. "We can hold Mr. Bunny. We'll still be twins, no matter what."

Mrs. Otis put the tallest kids in the back and the shortest kids in front. Elizabeth and I were in the middle. I reached for Mr. Bunny, but Amy held him tight. "He's scared," Amy said, nuzzling Mr. Bunny's face against hers.

If Amy wasn't going to let Elizabeth hold the bunny, Elizabeth would have nothing to cover her stain! She'd stick out like a big neon Band-Aid on a skinny pinky finger—a big neon Band-Aid with an unhappy face.

"Is everyone ready?" the photographer asked.

"Not yet," I said. Being a star was important, but my sister was even more important.

I ducked out and ran back to room 203. I found my leftover grape juice box and stuck in the straw. Then I squeezed it. Grape juice squirted all down my dress, so it was just like Elizabeth's. Smiling, I ran back to the auditorium.

"Wait," I heard Mrs. Otis saying as I made it to the door. "Where's Jessica?" The kids were all looking for me as if I were one of the lost hamsters. Charlie was on his knees, searching under the camera.

I ran into the room. "Here I am!"

Elizabeth's eyes popped open in surprise when she saw my dress. "Jessica, where'd you get that grape juice stain?" she asked.

"I poured it myself," I said with a grin. "Now we're twins again."

Elizabeth giggled. "And best friends forever."

"Hurry, line up," Mrs. Otis said. She gave me a funny look, but then she smiled. Our class scrambled back into place.

Elizabeth and I squeezed hands. The camera flashed and almost blinded us.

"Now for individual shots," the photographer said.

Lila went first. She took forever fixing her dress. *I guess she'll be the star of picture day after all,* I thought. But I didn't care about that anymore.

Then Winston slipped behind her and stuck his fingers up like bunny ears.

Everyone laughed. Poor Lila didn't even realize he'd done it.

Then Winston sat down on the stool.

"OK, say 'pepperoni pizza,'" the photographer said.

Winston started to say something else, but the cameraman snapped the shot first. Winston looked silly enough in his crazy shirt, but now his mouth was twisted too.

Eva was next.

"Say 'fuzzy pickles,'" the photographer said to Eva.

Eva smiled with her lips together so her missing tooth wouldn't show. But then Winston made a silly face at her. The flash went off right when Eva started to laugh. Her big smile showed off her missing tooth for the camera.

Then Elizabeth and I took our turns.

"I can't tell who is who," the photographer said. "You even have twin purple stains."

Elizabeth laughed. It was the strangest class picture day ever!

CHAPTER 12

The Pen Pals Write Back

A couple of weeks later Mrs. Otis tacked our class picture on the bulletin board next to the one from Alaska.

"Look at our picture," Elizabeth said.

I laughed. "Look at Tinkerbell. She's climbing up Mrs. Otis's arm!"

Lila didn't say anything. She was still sulking after seeing how Winston had ruined her picture.

Elizabeth laughed and opened the letter from her pen pal. "Did you read yours yet?" she asked me.

I shook my head and opened my letter.

Dear Jessica,

It looks like you sure have fun in your school. I wish we had hamsters for pets. It's hard to play with a moose. Your teacher looks cool. Mrs. Gazak would never let a hamster crawl on her.

I'm going to a big dogsled race soon. I hate that furry brown coat. My brother calls me a moose when I wear it.

You and your twin sister are pretty (but your big smile makes you look like a real movie star).

Your pen pal from Alaska,
Bob Burdett

"Well, what did he say?" Elizabeth asked.

I folded the letter and held it close to my chest. "Oh, not much. Just dumb stuff about dogsled racing."

Elizabeth laughed.

"And that I looked like a movie star," I said.

"See, our class picture wasn't so bad after all." Elizabeth smiled. "Maybe your pen pal isn't so bad either."

I nodded. "You're right about picture day, but Bob's still a *boy*."

Deep down, though, I wondered if Elizabeth might be right about both things. Of course, I would never tell her that. Some things you don't even tell your twin sister.

Just then Caroline came up behind us. "Guess what?" she asked.

I tried to ignore Caroline. She's always spreading gossip or talking behind people's backs. She was probably going to tease me about my pen pal.

"What?" Elizabeth asked, knowing Caroline wouldn't leave us alone until we heard what she had to say.

Caroline looked smug. "I heard

Mrs. Otis is retiring. She won't be our teacher anymore."

Elizabeth and I looked at each other. That couldn't be true. It had to be another of Caroline's rumors. But what if it wasn't?

Could our favorite teacher really be leaving Sweet Valley Elementary?

What will Elizabeth and Jessica do if Mrs. Otis retires? Find out in Sweet Valley Kids #70, **GOOD-BYE, MRS. OTIS.**

Elizabeth's Word Search

Elizabeth wrote down ten of her favorite words and names from the story. Then she hid each one either horizontally (side-to-side) or vertically (up-and-down) in the word search puzzle at the bottom of the page. Can you find all ten? Good luck!

ALASKA   MOOSEBOY
CAMERA   ORANGE
ESKIMO   PICTURE
GRIZZLY   STAIN
LAVA   VOLCANO

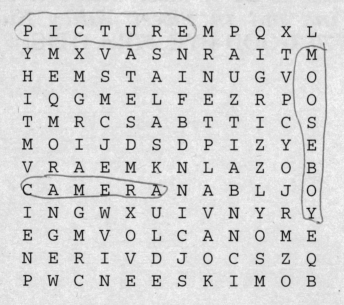

```
P I C T U R E M P Q X L
Y M X V A S N R A I T M
H E M S T A I N U G V O
I Q G M E L F E Z R P O
T M R C S A B T T I C S
M O I J D S D P I Z Y E
V R A E M K N L A Z O B
C A M E R A N A B L J O
I N G W X U I V N Y R Y
E G M V O L C A N O M E
N E R I V D J O C S Z Q
P W C N E E S K I M O B
```

Jessica's Crossword Puzzle

Jessica remembered ten things that happened in the story. But after she wrote them out, she erased a word or name from each sentence!

When you figure out what the missing word or name is, fill in the blanks. Then you can write the missing word in the matching crossword spaces!

Can you get all ten words right without peeking back at the story? Good luck!

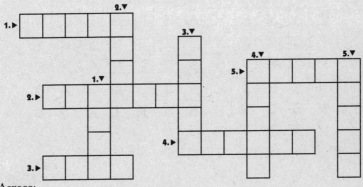

Across:

1. The teacher in Alaska was named Mrs. _ _ _ _ _.
2. Elizabeth found out that Alaskan Eskimos came from _ _ _ _ _ _ _ _
3. Some boys wore _ _ _ _ around their necks when they dressed up.
4. Elizabeth wanted to wear _ _ _ _ _ _ on picture day, but Jessica didn't.
5. Jessica hoped the surprise would be a _ _ _ _ _ party.

Down:

1. Charlie knocked over a jar of _ _ _ _ paint.
2. Julie skinned her _ _ _ _ playing jump rope.
3. Steven wanted to wear ripped _ _ _ _ _ on picture day.
4. Lila wore a _ _ _ _ _ necklace.
5. Eva lost her tooth in an _ _ _ _ _ _.

TURN THE PAGE FOR ANSWERS ➤

Answers

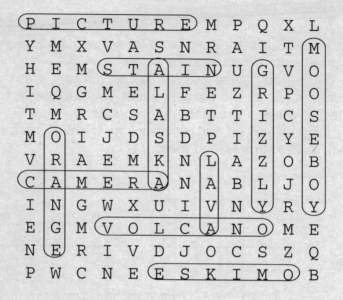

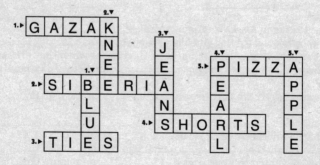

SIGN UP FOR THE SWEET VALLEY HIGH® FAN CLUB!

Hey, girls! Get all the gossip on Sweet Valley High's® most popular teenagers when you join our fantastic Fan Club! As a member, you'll get all of this really cool stuff:

- Membership Card with your own personal Fan Club ID number
- A Sweet Valley High® Secret Treasure Box
- Sweet Valley High® Stationery
- Official Fan Club Pencil (for secret note writing!)
- Three Bookmarks
- A "Members Only" Door Hanger
- Two Skeins of J. & P. Coats® Embroidery Floss with flower barrette instruction leaflet
- Two editions of *The Oracle* newsletter
- Plus exclusive Sweet Valley High® product offers, special savings, contests, and much more!

Be the first to find out what Jessica & Elizabeth Wakefield are up to by joining the Sweet Valley High® Fan Club for the one-year membership fee of only $6.25 each for U.S. residents, $8.25 for Canadian residents (U.S. currency). Includes shipping & handling.

Send a check or money order (do not send cash) made payable to "Sweet Valley High® Fan Club" along with this form to:

SWEET VALLEY HIGH® FAN CLUB, BOX 3919-B, SCHAUMBURG, IL 60168-3919

NAME_____
(Please print clearly)

ADDRESS_____

CITY_____ STATE _____ ZIP_____
(Required)

AGE _____ BIRTHDAY_____ /_____ /_____

Offer good while supplies last. Allow 6-8 weeks after check clearance for delivery. Addresses without ZIP codes cannot be honored. Offer good in USA & Canada only. Void where prohibited by law.
©1993 by Francine Pascal   LCI-1383-123